ALPHA Geek

NEW YORK TIMES and *USA TODAY* BESTSELLING AUTHOR

MILLY TAIDEN

Alpha Geek

Published By

Latin Goddess Press

Winter Springs, FL 32708

http://millytaiden.com

Cover by Willsin Rowe

Edited by: Tina Winograd

Formatting by After Glows Publishing Services

August 2016

ALPHA GEEK

Lioness shifter Scarlett Milan hates that she wants her boss more than her next breath. All she thinks about is how his black-rimmed glasses and bow tie are sexier on him than any other man. But since he's human, she's afraid she could break him, even kill him, during a night of wild sex.

Knox Daniels, wimpy bean counter, has lusted after Scarlett since the moment he met her. The fact she's his best friend's little sister has stopped all dirty thoughts. Well, almost. After he breaks up with his girlfriend, getting his hands on Scarlett is the first thing on his to-do list. Being murdered was not.

A vicious attack almost kills Knox, but science comes to the rescue. Now he's no longer the weak human Scarlett was afraid to touch. Actually, no one knows what he is except possessive, aggressive, and demanding she be his. They'll have to team up to keep him alive while figuring out if he's a deranged killer or just the most powerful alpha ever known.

—For my geek-loving daughter, Angelina

This geek is all yours. I love you!

ONE

Scarlett Milan was going to kill her boss. She would watch his life drain from the slashes she'd leave on his neck. Then, she'd lick her paws and finally get some peace.

"Scarlett?" Knox Daniels' voice made the lioness want to purr. Damn, stupid animal. What the fuck was wrong with her?

"Yes, Knox?" She turned to face him, swiveling in her chair. He wore those black-rimmed glasses he needed or he'd never see his own hand in front of his face. A blue dress shirt and a bow tie. Yeah, a bow tie. Not even a regular tie. For an investment banker, he was such a geek. He even had a frickin' pocket protector.

Did her annoying lioness care he was a geek? No, she did not. Her bitch of a lioness wanted her boss. She cared he had eyes a softer brown than milk chocolate. Except Scarlett didn't like her boss. She couldn't. She'd probably break him in bed. Fucking hell.

Why the hell was she thinking of herself and Knox in bed? Why?

"I…I was hoping…"

She raised her brows and watched him tug at his bow tie. Dammit. Once again she had to suppress a purr from her feline and shut the animal up. "You were hoping?"

He cleared his throat. She stared deeply into his beautiful brown eyes and squeezed her legs together. Goddamn, he was so sexy.

He glanced down at her chest. The scent of his own arousal made it damn hard for her to push her lioness back. The bitch wanted to strip him to just the bow tie and the glasses while she fucked him.

He visibly gulped and glanced away from her low-cut neckline. She could say she hadn't chosen that dress to purposely taunt him, but that was a lie. She knew he wanted her and hated that he was her boss. Hated that he was oblivious to her desires and hated that he disliked wanting her.

More than anything, she hated that he was human and she could never truly go wild with him.

Not to mention how boring he was. He never did anything. Spent days and nights in the office and the only reason she knew he liked women was because she smelled how he wanted her.

Even with all that, the man had a girlfriend. It boggled the mind. Okay, it really didn't. Those gorgeous eyes behind those black-rimmed spectacles. That clean-shaven look and his hair always in place did things to her that no naked man ever had. Fucking hormones! He never crossed the line when it came to Scarlett. No. It was all work with him. All about making sure she was busy doing the most boring job on the planet.

She really needed to find a new job.

No, you don't. Mate. Mate. Mate. Argh! If her lioness weren't so hard-headed, she'd have been able to leave this job, but no. The fact that she liked being near Knox kept Scarlett from quitting. She didn't know why her stupid cat kept thinking of him as her mate, but no man she could break in bed could be her mate. No fucking way.

"Knox?" she repeated, pulling him out of whatever daydream he was having with his work. "What were you hoping?"

"That you would come to the company party

this weekend."

She saw desire in his eyes. Her pussy went slick. Thank god, he couldn't smell her or things would get real fucking awkward. "I'm not sure if I can, but I'll do my best."

He smiled and her nipples tightened. She had to be going into heat. It was the only explanation to how suddenly she couldn't get enough of his voice or the way his dark eyes roamed her face until he stopped at her lips. She licked her lips and was rewarded with him clearing his throat. Her cat purred and she had to cough to hide the sound.

"I'm going to have dinner with Lisa," he said, tugging his bow tie again. "I'll see you tomorrow at the party."

If he mentioned his girlfriend one more time, she might hiss. She'd yet to meet the woman, but her lioness hated her guts as it was. Not to mention she'd seen a photo of him and her in the paper at some swanky charity thing.

"Have you talked to her father about those deposits?" she asked.

"I left him a message. Once I hear back from him, I'll know where to go from there."

"Hopefully, he can tell you where all that money came from since you're supposed to be the one handling his accounts. I don't get how someone can buy a company with capital that wasn't there. Where did it come from?"

"Don't worry about that stuff, I'll figure it out."

She waved him out of the office, hating that he was leaving, but she took a breath and slipped her heels off. Time to relax.

She picked up the phone and dialed her sister-in-law, Shani. Her brother's wife had invited her for dinner and she was taking her up on it. First, because Scarlett loved Shani's cooking. Second, because she was dying to hold her newest nephew, Max.

"Hello, darling!" Shani answered. The sound of kids laughing in the background made it hard to hear her.

"I'm coming. Be there in half an hour."

"Wonderful. I made your favorite. Nick is off protecting some movie star so we won't be eating with him tonight."

Scarlett's brother owned a security company. Thankfully, Shani was incredibly understanding that her husband was constantly protecting some rich guy or another. Scarlett was happy to help Shani with the kids when Nick wasn't around.

She went into Knox's office to put a file on his desk and the scent of him made her lioness crazy.

She went around his desk and sat on his chair.

Pressing her body into the cushion, she inhaled hard. Fuck, it smelled just like him. He'd left a handkerchief on his desk. It was folded neatly into a square with his initials embroidered on a corner.

Her body throbbed and she couldn't get the image of him in the fucking bow tie and his sexy eyes looking at her out of her mind. She needed to get laid. Fast.

TWO

Knox sat in his car waiting for Lisa to show up at the restaurant. She was always late. He should just end things with her, but every time he mentioned dating other people, she started the waterworks, and he had no idea how to shut it up other than to tell her to forget it.

His cell phone chirped. An alarm that someone was in his office blinked to life. A few key strokes and he was accessing the remote camera he'd installed in his office. Since he was working with Lisa's father's accounts and buying a new company, he'd been specific about security. He'd taken extra measures to ensure his locked up paperwork wasn't tampered with.

The camera gave a clear image of his desk. His cock went hard as he watched Scarlett, his sexy as hell assistant, sit in his chair. He glanced around the dark parking lot. His was the only car there. Most people parked in areas closer to the main road, but he liked not worrying about someone scratching his Bugatti.

The car was his one gift to himself. There had been no reason for it, either. He'd just gone out one day and bought it. His gaze went back to Scarlett in his chair.

She leaned back and lifted her legs, her skirt falling to either side of her hips. He straightened in his seat. What was she doing?

When his friend Nick had asked him to give his little sister a job, Knox hadn't expected Scarlett. Hell, in all the years he'd known the lion, he'd never met Nick's sister. Then they'd had dinner at Nick's place, and Knox had never been the same again.

On her first day at the job, his tongue almost fell out of his mouth when she walked in the door.

Her gorgeous peachy skin alone caught his attention. But the full package? Those curves, the tattoos, and the long black curls made his dick hard enough to hammer nails. When she spoke, her soft throaty voice did him in. He'd actually gone to the bathroom to jerk off just thinking of her voice.

He'd been disgusted with himself. This was Nick's little sister. Though nothing was little about her. Not her sumptuous curves and not her breasts. Certainly not that gorgeous ass. One of his favorite things about her was the way her eyes glowed a sexy gold that he knew meant her wild side was near.

It wasn't that he was intimidated by her. Not really. He just respected the fact she was his friend's sister. That and she was out of his fucking league. The short dresses she wore with the low cut tops that showed off her breasts drove him fucking crazy. He should tell her to be more professional, but who the hell was he kidding? He loved wondering what she might wear every day.

He continued looking at her on the phone's screen. Her sexy lips formed a pout. He'd already learned all her facial expressions. That look on her face meant she was frustrated. He wondered why. He ate up the image of her sitting at his desk. She was so goddamned sexy.

His cock hurt, and he found himself stroking it over his pants. It wasn't enough. He watched her slide a hand between her legs. Shit! Was she really going to? Yes, she was. He hadn't even realized he'd pulled his dick out of his pants until he glanced down and saw it in his grip.

For fuck's sake, he hadn't had sex in too goddamned long.

Lisa wanted to, but every time he tried to do anything, his dick went limp, refusing to work. It was embarrassing as hell. All he had to do was think about Scarlett and he went instantly hard. If he didn't know better, he'd think she was a witch instead of a lioness.

He'd decided tonight was a good night to end things with Lisa. He'd break up with her even if she cried. He was done with her. That decision made allowed him to watch Scarlett guilt free.

Scarlett pushed her panties to the side and he tapped an icon that zoomed in on the image of her. The camera he'd installed was the best and damn expensive. He realized now it had been worth its weight in gold. It gave him the clearest image of her.

She yanked down the neckline of her dress, revealing her hard-pointed nipples. His mouth watered. Beads of moisture gathered at the tip of his dick. He used it to lubricate his cock and jerk harder. At the moment, he could give two fucks how hard he was handling his dick.

Her shoe-less feet pressed at the edge of his desk. She leaned the chair back and fondled her pussy with her right hand while tugging on her nipples with her left.

"Fuck, that's a beautiful sight."

She increased her speed, her eyes closed. Her

pink tongue swiped over her full lips as if she were getting them ready to suck his dick. Yes. His dick. Because this was his fantasy, and he'd give his left testicle to make it a reality.

As she increased in speed, so did he. He jerked in tandem with her circles on her clit. Her pussy gleamed pink and so fucking perfect, he could imagine being the one in the room with her, pressing his fingers to her clit. She cracked her lids open and the golden glow was there.

"Look at me," he whispered to the phone. She glanced up at the lamp in his office, to the very spot he'd had the camera hidden. It almost looked like she was looking right at him, and he loved it.

He jerked harder, watching her chest rise and fall with her breathing. She tugged on a nipple and tapped on her clit. Her hips rose off the chair. Another tap and she bit her bottom lip.

He watched her toes curl on the desk. Her breathing increased in speed. Wetness dripped from her slit, and she slid two fingers into her pussy and gripped the armrest as she came.

He continued to jerk and when he saw her grab his handkerchief and wipe her pussy juices with it, he fucking lost it. He grabbed at the napkin in his cup holder and covered the head of his cock as he came.

Streams of cum landed on the napkin, a napkin

he wished at that moment was her slick, hot sex. He milked his cock, the image in his mind of her wiping her pussy with his handkerchief, one he'd never wash. Fuck. Her face had been priceless.

His phone buzzed in his hand, interrupting his video feed, and he almost had a heart attack. He cleaned up and put his dick away. The last thing he needed was someone to catch him doing that shit.

Lisa. Fuck, he'd forgotten all about her. "Lisa?"

"Where are you? I've been waiting at the restaurant for at least two minutes."

He bit down the urge to send her to hell. "I'm coming." He wasn't lying.

"Well, hurry up!"

Tonight. Definitely tonight. He was at the end of his fucking rope with her.

THREE

Scarlett knocked at Shani's door with a smile. She'd been naughty in Knox's office and he'd never know. Oh, he might find the dirty handkerchief in his drawer and assume it'd been used, but she'd know. After her little self-pleasure moment in his office, she'd ended up using his private shower.

"You look like the cat that ate the canary." Shani laughed. "What did you do?"

Scarlett shrugged. "Nothing. I'm just happy it's Friday."

Shani raised a brow, bouncing little Max in her arms. "Do I look like I was born yesterday?"

She giggled and wiggled her fingers, ready to

take baby Max for herself.

Her lioness purred the moment she had the little cub in her arms. Man, she wanted babies so badly. If only her damn cat wasn't obsessed with Mr. Geek and would look at other shifter males. No way in hell was she mating him.

"So, how was work?" Shani asked in the living room.

"Hey, where are Taylor and Tiana?"

"The twins are asleep," Shani said and raised a glass of wine filled with fruit punch in a toast. "The only one awake is alpha baby over here."

She glanced at Max and fell in love with his big brown eyes. They reminded him of Knox's sexy chocolate eyes. The baby gurgled and gave her a toothless grin. She hugged him and inhaled the scent of baby and lion cub. Both her human maternal instinct and her lioness sighed.

Her biological clock was hammering the need for kids over her head and she wasn't even mated.

"Scarlett!" Shani exclaimed. "Are you listening to me? I asked how was work."

"Same old." She grinned, unable to suppress the memory of what she did in Knox's office.

"Doesn't look like it to me. You look guilty." Shani sighed. "Remember that Knox is a good guy. Your brother had to talk to him to get you a job."

She knew that. Knox had known Nick all through college and helped Nick learn to build his money, to make his wealth work for him. Heck, Nick, Shani, and the kids were set up for life thanks to Knox.

The man was a genius when it came to the stock market and finances. She bounced Max on her lap. "I know. I'm doing my job. I chose to stop working at Nick's security business because I got tired of getting shot at by stupid humans. Hunting and capturing the bad guys was exciting, but my lioness wanted out of that kind of business."

Shani nodded. "You lost your patience a lot."

"Yeah, well, there were a lot of really dumb shifters that wanted to be protected and did the exact shit we told them not to do so they wouldn't put themselves in danger. A person can only do so much before realizing these morons like the attention."

She'd quit on Nick. He had been so understanding, telling her he understood. The truth was once she realized she would rather hurt some of those clients herself than protect them, she knew there was a problem.

"I do my job when it comes to Knox. He has no

complaints." She was the one having a hard time not riding him on his office chair. She wanted to yank down his pants, scratch his chest and watch his black-rimmed glasses fog up from the heat they'd create. But Knox was human. And she didn't have it in her to go there with him.

Do it. Just one time. Just once.

"Are you excited?" Shani refilled her fruit punch and passed a glass to Scarlett, who raised a brow. "Don't look at me like that. If I have to drink fruit punch, so do you."

"What is it you think I should be excited about?" she said, rocking Max back and forth. He'd gone quiet and his eyes started drooping.

"Scarlett, really?" Shani shook her head. "The party Knox is having this weekend. He's invited every employee and client."

"Oh, that. Meh. I'm not sure if I'm going," she said softly and lowered her face to Max's and brushed a kiss on his dark head.

"You have to go!" Shani exclaimed.

She glanced up and met her sister-in-law's serious gaze. "Why?"

Shani turned away and then gave her a guilty look. "We already said you would."

"What? Why?"

"Knox looked so excited to have you there. It

was hard saying we didn't know, so we said yes for you."

"Shani!"

Shani winced. "Sorry. But yes, now you have to go."

"Well, at least I'll have you guys as company." Shani glanced down at her glass. "Oh, come on! You're not going? What the hell will I do there if you guys aren't coming?"

"Mingle? Maybe meet a single man? Heck, you never know, you might meet your mate."

She growled and stood. "I'm putting this cutie pie to bed."

Once she laid the baby down, she stood by his crib and watched him. Knox and his geeky glasses and bow tie came to her mind. Her lioness purred and whined, pushing at her skin.

Mine! Mine! Mine!

No! No! No! The damn feline was not getting the picture. Knox wasn't her mate. He was a weak human she could mash in the throes of sex. All she had to do was scratch him and he'd be mortally wounded or end up in the hospital.

She couldn't live with herself if she killed him. *So change him*. That wasn't guaranteed to work. He could die. She wasn't taking that chance.

FOUR

Scarlett got out of her car and sighed. No backing out now. Not when she'd spent all day looking for the perfect costume for this shindig. Only Knox would come up with a Halloween party weeks too early.

She'd finally decided on the slave girl Princess Leia from Star Wars. So what if she had a lot more in the curves department than the original Leia. She still pulled it off quite nicely if she went by the looks she got as she entered Knox's haunted mansion.

She didn't know how Knox rented the place, but they'd done a freaking amazing job with the décor. Her favorite part was the cavemen waiters walking around, handing out glasses of champagne.

Some guy dressed as a vampire tried to get her attention. She hissed at him. The face he made almost had her in stitches. This might be fun after all.

She looked all over but didn't see anyone dressed as a lawyer or judge, which was what she'd overheard Knox saying he'd dress up as.

"Do you want to dance?" a guy in a police officer costume asked.

She sipped the drink she'd just gotten and whispered by his ear, "Do you want your balls up your ass?"

He lifted his hands and backed away slowly. The crowds got thicker and once the music started pumping, she knew she had to get out of there. She walked out a side door down a wraparound balcony toward the back of the mansion.

She stopped when she smelled Knox. Where was he? Glancing around in the darkness, she didn't see him. The wind shifted and she hurried farther down the balcony. She stopped at a set of glass doors. He was in there.

She should leave. What if he wanted to be alone? *He doesn't. He wants you*. Great. Her lioness was losing her fucking mind again. She'd go inside, casually say hi and then hit the road. Not like he'd notice her being gone while everyone partied in the grand salon.

The cool knob turned silently under her hand. She strolled inside quietly. The décor resembled what one would find in a five-star hotel suite. Must be a guest room.

It looked like a man was readying the room for someone. He pushed the vase of flowers to the center of the dresser. Her gaze ate him up from head to toe. Oh, wow. Oh, hell. Her lioness purred with need. It would be damn impossible to leave him alone now.

"Knox?"

He turned to face her and she gulped.

"You made it."

Yeah. She'd made it all right. Her gaze took in his finger combed hair, the black-rimmed glasses, but that's all he had of his usual Knox. He was naked from the waist up. A red Superman symbol was painted on his chest and navy pants dressed his legs. Form fitting pants. The kind that outlined his very large package.

She licked her lips while still staring at his cock and realized how that must look to him. Her gaze shot up to his. She'd never been into superheroes, but at that moment, she could totally see herself wanting to screw this Superman's brains out.

"Are you okay?"

He gave her a sinful smile she wanted to kiss off his lips. "Now that you're here I am."

Whoa! This was getting rocky. "Where's Lisa? Did you talk to her father yet?"

"I haven't. I know he's here somewhere. I'll get to him before the end of the party. The more I look into his accounts and where he's getting capital to buy his business, the more I know something weird is going on."

She nodded. "What, um…what about Lisa. Is she here?"

He took a step toward her. "I don't know. I broke things off last night, but her father is my client so he and her were both invited to the party."

Why did he have to tell her that? The knowledge he was in a relationship was the only thing keeping her on a leash of sorts. More steps. He got closer and the scent of his lust started to make her dizzy. He wanted her big time.

"I'm sure you'll find someone else," she mumbled, staggering back. She had to get away from him. Her self-control was at its limit.

"I already did." He took his glasses off and tossed them on a chair near him.

Uh. Oh. He rushed forward, grabbed her by

the forearms, and pushed her against the glass door.

"Knox, what are you doing?"

"What I should have done months ago," he muttered. "Taking what I want."

There wasn't a chance to tell him to stop. To warn him he was a weak human and she could break him. He took her lips and did something no man had ever done. He owned them. He kissed her with a forceful dominance she hadn't seen in any human in her life.

A blaze of fire lit her core. He raked his hands down her body, stroking and grasping her flesh. Power was behind his strong caresses. He cupped her breasts, sucking her tongue and grinding his cock into her.

She was glad she'd worn sky-high heels. It put them at the same height and allowed her to cushion his cock in the V of her crotch.

She curled a leg around his waist and ground her pussy on his erection. All that stood between them was the thin material of her bottom and his pants. Both easily disposed of.

Her lioness snarled, wanting to bite, but she held her back. This wasn't her dance. Scarlett was letting him kiss her. She'd been dying to taste Knox. If this was the only way she'd get that, her lioness would be pissed but out of the way.

She glided her fingers over his muscled, thin shoulders, down his narrow arms, to his abs. Good lord, the man was tight. He had to work out like crazy. Who would've known he hid that under those suits?

He broke off their kiss, his mouth immediately attaching to her neck, licking and sucking. Heat triggered in her pussy. She ached to have him. Raking her nails over his shoulders, she kept reminding herself to not scratch him. To control her cat.

With a swift tug, her bra top was pulled down and he had one of her nipples in his mouth. Shudders raced down her back. Her breasts grew full and heavy. It wasn't smart to let him touch her, to let him have her, but she wanted him, too.

Pushing both her breasts together, he licked and sucked one nipple and then the other, going back and forth. Her belly quivered as need increased to a desperate inferno.

"God, Scarlett. You're so fucking beautiful."

FIVE

Scarlett had never been one to get caught up with words, but hearing him say that, knowing he wasn't lying, made her even wetter.

He slipped a hand into the waist of her golden panties, spread her pussy lips, and dipped in.

"Oh god, yes!" Her pussy throbbed, grasping at nothing.

He bit down on her nipple, the pain shooting shards of pleasure to her sex. "Baby, you're drenched. So slick and hot."

She gripped his hair and let him touch her everywhere. "Knox..."

He met her gaze, his face and lips so close. She

wanted to push him to his knees and tell him to make a meal out of her. "Tell me what you want, Scarlett. I'll give it to you."

He would. She knew he would and wasn't passing it up, but first, she'd make sure she wasn't a danger to him.

"Who's room is this?"

"I was hoping you'd stay here for the night."

Oh, hell. She hadn't come with that in mind, but now that he mentioned it, she really liked this idea. "Why were you here alone?"

He licked his lips while staring at her mouth. "I was trying to make the room perfect before I went looking for you."

She glanced at the four-poster bed then back to him. "Tie me to the bed."

He jerked back as if she'd slapped him. "What?"

"Tie me to the bed," she repeated. "It'll keep me from hurting you."

He shook his head. "You won't—"

"Do it or I leave." She tugged on the scarves dangling from her see-through skirt. Two tore off easily. She handed them to him and nodded.

He pressed his lips into a thin line. She fully expected him to argue with her, but he didn't.

Instead, he led her to the bed and watched her lie in the center. The scarves were flimsy, but she wasn't expecting them to act like chains. They were only there as a reminder that she needed to keep her animal in check.

One hand tied, he went around the massive bed and did the other. Then he ambled to the foot of the bed, his gaze on her body. Her lioness purred and she let the soft noise out, allowing him to hear it. She tugged on the binds. They held when she didn't put too much pressure on them.

He crawled up the bed, lifting her high-heeled foot to his face. A soft kiss was placed by the edge of her shoe strap near her ankle. Moisture gathered at her pussy, need making it almost impossible to lie still. She breathed deeply, the sound of each inhale loud in her ears.

"Knox," she whispered.

"Give me a second. I've been dying to touch every part of you." He placed her foot on his shoulder and caressed both legs as he moved up the bed. The look on his face when he shoved the rest of her see-through skirt to the side made her squirm. "How do I get it off?"

Dangling chains and intricate metal links made her skirt and panty set look a lot harder to get off than they were. "Zipper on each side. Button unclips the skirt." He quickly found both and unzipped, unclipped, and pulled the set off without needing to move her. She lifted her other leg and placed it over his shoulder.

He glanced away from her pussy folds and up to her face. "You're so wet."

She licked her lips. "I taste good, too. Try it."

He stroked a finger up and down her pussy, coating it in her wetness. The same finger went up to his lips. She watched him curl his tongue around it. Breaths sounded harder in her ears.

"You're right," he murmured. "I want more."

Her chest squeezed with every inch his head lowered until she couldn't get air into her lungs. He blew on her clit and she had to clench her teeth to keep from growling.

"This is the one time I wish I was a shifter," he said to her pussy. "So I can smell you deeper." He swiped his tongue over her aching flesh. "So I can taste you better."

"Fuck!" Men didn't say shit like that to her. She tried to grab his hair to shove him into her crotch, but her arms stopped midway, pulled back by the bindings. "Lick my pussy, Knox."

He raised his head and grinned. "I'm starting to like those scarves."

She growled and let her arms drop, raising her hips off the bed to bring her pussy to his mouth. "Please."

"Since you asked nicely." He went back in, flicking his tongue over her heat, sucking hard at her clit, making her burn from the inside with pleasure.

She crossed her ankles over the back of his head, holding him hostage with her legs. He didn't seem to mind, he groaned that she tasted so good. Her pussy creamed with every lick.

"God!"

The pressure at her clit became unbearable. Her lioness pushed so hard to get out, she worried for once, she might lose control. The animal rolled under her skin, making her hot, tight, and desperate.

He caressed up and down her pussy with his fingers. Two went into her channel, driving deeply and pulling back to press at her G-spot. Another finger pushed at the rim of her ass, coating it with her wetness before finally diving in.

"Yes! Yes! Yes!" Her voice turned deeper, rougher.

"You are so fucking sexy," he whispered and lapped at her clit. He suckled hard, grazing his teeth on her stiff pleasure center at the same time he drove his fingers in and out of her pussy and ass.

SIX

Scarlett couldn't breathe. Tension unfurled inside her, breaking all speed records. In thirty seconds flat, she was thrashing on the bed, her heels digging into his back as she came hard on his mouth. A loud scream tore from her throat. She blinked the spots away from her vision. God. She'd never realized a human man could make her that hot.

She was still shaking when his pants came down and his cock moved to her entrance. He slipped the same fingers he'd had in her pussy into her mouth. "Taste yourself." He rubbed his fingers on her tongue. "See how sweet you are. My cock wants to taste you now."

Lord. This human might be the exception to the rule. How was a geek this fucking dirty?

He thrust hard, in one smooth glide he was balls deep inside her. She moaned, his fingers still in her mouth. She continued to suck them, her flavor lingering on her tongue.

He filled her tight heat, drawing gasps and moans as he fucked her. Every thrust had her wishing she could touch him. His arms and shoulder muscles bunched as he tensed with every plunge into her sex.

Gripping the bedding, she ignored the sound of material tearing. She knew she'd done that, but her focus was on his face and the way he looked deeply into her eyes with every thrust.

"I've never wanted a woman like I want you."

He yanked her top down, spilling her breasts and cupping one into his palm. Leaning forward, he lifted her ass off the bed, her legs still over his shoulders, and sucked a nipple into his mouth. His cool tongue curled around the tip and then his blunt teeth bit down, making her pussy suck hard on his cock.

"Fuck, baby. Do that again," he ground out through clenched teeth.

Another bite on her nipple and she did. A full body shudder shot down her back and straight to her clit, her pussy grasping at his dick.

He moved her legs off his shoulders to curl around his waist, driving deeper into her. She licked her lips. "Kiss me, Knox."

He didn't hesitate. His lips came crashing over hers. Thirsty. Hungry. Desperate. Her mind shut down as his scent filled her senses. Their tongues twined, slid and caressed. He took her breath and gave his back, his cock still pounding into her.

Then he pressed a finger to her clit as he rammed her. She tried to hang on, but her feline wasn't listening. There was an overload of sensations and she fell over the edge.

Mounting pleasure washed over her with his continued thrusts. Her pussy tightened around his cock. He took the scream from her lips, swallowing it as he continued to plunge inside her.

Then he slowed, his lips came off her and he stared deeply into her eyes. "This is only the beginning, Scarlett."

His head dropped, his shoulder within reach of her lips. Her lioness roared. This was her chance to take him. To make him hers. He belonged to her.

Mine! Mine! Mine!

She sucked on his shoulder, her teeth elongating into canines. Then she remembered why she was tied up. She wasn't mating him.

There was no way she'd be responsible for hurting him. If he didn't take the change, her bite could kill him.

So she nibbled on his slick shoulder, not hard enough to break skin, but enough to make him come inside her. To make her moan and come again from the feel of his cum filling her channel.

When she tried to push her lioness back, the animal fought her for control. This wasn't her first rodeo. Her lioness knew Scarlett was the stronger of the two. Yet, at that moment, her animal tried to break loose and bite Knox. No! She couldn't have that. She steeled herself against the animal, but in her aroused state, it was hard to wrap her mind around not wanting him for a mate when she truly did. If she didn't do something soon, he'd be bitten, scratched, and possibly dead in the next thirty seconds.

She tore the scarves off the bed and did the only thing she could think of: she shoved Knox off and ran. Her shift came quickly as she crashed through the glass door and ran into the waiting forest.

SEVEN

Knox got up from the floor and ran to the broken glass door. She was gone. His cock was still wet from her pussy juices and though he'd just come inside her, fuck!, he wanted more. Wanted her. He zipped up his pants and continued to stare into the forest. He clenched his teeth and picked up his glasses from the chair he'd tossed them on.

Two of the dozens of guards he'd hired to oversee the event showed up. They saw the door and him.

"Everything's fine," he said before they went looking for her. The last thing he wanted was some other man finding his woman because she was his, whether she agreed with him or not.

"Sir, did you want us to block off this area?"

He nodded and walked out the broken door, carefully avoiding shards. The men dispersed to find the supplies needed to clear out the glass and shut down the shattered door. Thank goodness the men worked for Nick and were used to that kind of stuff. A busted door was nothing when someone was trying to kill a musical idol.

Knox pulled out his phone and sent Shani a text. He wanted to make sure someone let him know when Scarlett showed up. And if she was okay.

He marched toward the front of the house when he saw someone being dragged into the trees near his house. He rushed forward, glancing around to see if any of the security he hired were back. None of them were around. Waiting might be wisest, but he didn't want to take chances. What if someone needed help?

He rushed into the woods, trying to hear for the couple he'd seen. Leaves crunched under the pressure of his boots. He should've grabbed a jacket before coming out. It was nippy.

"Let me go!"

The sound was faint, but he ran toward it. The woman's voice sounded panicked and scared.

"You're coming with me, princess."

"I said let go!"

Knox ran faster toward the voices until they got closer and closer. He passed a tree and came up on a man dragging a woman he knew all too well.

"Lisa?" So she had shown up, even after he'd told her he couldn't date her any longer but would be happy to keep her father on as a client.

Lisa turned to him, her eyes filled with horror. "Knox, get help. I don't want to be some guy's play thing."

The guy was big with large muscles and a bald head. He laughed at Knox. "Get the hell out of here before you get your face damaged."

"You heard him. Get out of here, puny human," said a voice behind Knox.

"Maybe he wants to play," a third guy said. He was the biggest with a long scar on the side of his face from left eye to upper lip.

The other two guys closed in on him. He pressed the number one button on his cell phone that should bring him immediate help. His guards would be there soon.

Scar face marched over to Lisa and squeezed her face in his hands. "You'll be mine tonight."

"Get away from me!" she screeched. "I'm not interested in being your anything."

Knox took three steps forward, but scar face turned golden eyes at him. "The human doesn't get it. I think he has a death wish."

"Leave her alone," he said and pressed the button on his phone again. Where the fuck were the guards?

"I think you're right, Mike," the guy who had Lisa let go and came around to Knox's side. "He does have a death wish."

Scar face yanked Lisa into his arms, his fingers digging into her side as he ignored her struggles and kissed her.

She screamed for Knox. He should have waited. He knew that. But instinct won out and the need to protect was one he couldn't fight. He tried to run to the guy, but the two guys grabbed him. They dragged him forward to the scar man.

His features changed, face elongating and hands turning into claws. "Then death it shall be."

It took Knox a second to realize what he was saying. By the time he did, the guy was tearing up his chest with a single swing of his claws. Knox glanced down. Blood seeped from his chest wounds. He didn't feel pain. Heat centered at his chest.

The other two let him go. He took the last few steps in a hurry and tried to pull Lisa out of the guy's grasp. He dug his claws into Knox's shoulder and yanked hard, stripping the arm to near bone.

He fell to the ground. Pain radiated in his chest. He couldn't feel his arm. Lisa and the man grabbing her turned fuzzy in his view. His glasses were gone. "Lisa…"

"Knox, don't die. I need you to help me!"

Knox opened his mouth to say something, but his tongue felt heavy. He couldn't speak. His vision tunneled, black closing in from the edges. He wanted to apologize to her that this happened at his party. The last thing he saw before everything turned dark was Lisa spitting on scar guy and him lifting a clawed hand and going for her face.

Scarlett ran into the bedroom where they had Knox in the mansion. Her stomach was going to toss out everything she ate the day before. Seeing as she hadn't a thing right before Knox's party and definitely nothing right after, she didn't think she'd vomit much. Nick had called her as he headed for the mansion when Knox was found. She'd hauled ass and got there as quickly as she could, not twenty minutes after the call.

"Nick," she said hastily in the bedroom.

A piercing scream from the bed made her stop and wince. Knox was chained with huge links to the wall behind the headboard. She tried to run to him, but Nick grasped her arm and stopped her.

"He's transitioning."

"Into what?"

"Wolf," Nick said. "I hope he is, anyway."

She met his gaze, her heart thumping so hard, she could barely hear anything else. "What happened? Who did this?"

Nick shook his head. "I don't know. My men didn't scent anyone in the area. They found him like this. Dying."

"Alone?" She gulped and took a step toward the bed, her gut clenching with fear.

"We scented a female, but there was no sign of her in the area," one of the guards said.

She watched Knox thrash, his face pale, and his chest and arm covered in blood. "There has to be something we can do." She turned to Nick. "Do something!"

Nick pressed his lips together. "What do you want me to do, Scarlett? He's past what I can do for him. Even if I bit him now, there's no chance he'd take a lion. He's already struggling against a wolf. In his condition, there's very little hope for him."

She ran for the bed, ignoring those watching and grabbed Knox's chained hand in her own. "Knox?"

A loud growl sounded from him followed by a

scream filled with so much pain, she choked back tears. "Knox, please. You have to fight to stay alive. Let the animal connect with you."

Another scream and mumble of something she didn't understand.

"Nick, what about Zeke?" Shani asked from the back of the room. "He's been working on something."

"We don't know if that would help or make things worse," Nick told her.

Scarlett turned to Nick. "Who's Zeke?"

"An old college friend of mine and Knox's. He's a scientist working on curing human diseases with shifter blood."

Shani cleared her throat and took Nick's arm. "Zeke mentioned the last time he came to dinner that when one of his smallest lab rats was injured by the office cat, he'd injected his newest serum into the animal and it had healed."

"Call him!" Scarlett screamed.

"We don't know if that would work on a human, much less one this close to death," Nick stated.

"Don't say that! He's not going to die. I won't let him," she screamed.

Shani's eyes filled with tears. "I'm sorry, Scarlett."

"Call him, Nick. Please," she cried, wiping angry tears from her cheeks. "Call him or I swear I'll scour this city until I find him."

Nick growled. "Fine. But I make no promises."

By the time Zeke showed up, almost an hour later, Knox was barely hanging on. The screams had subsided. She'd covered his injuries with ointment and gauze bandages. It made her feel she was helping somehow.

"Holy Toledo, what the hell happened exactly?" Zeke, a scrawny guy with giant Coke bottle glasses asked. He wore a Hans Solo T-shirt with a pair of black jeans a size too large.

"He was attacked by a wolf shifter," Nick growled. "I already told you this."

Zeke raised his hands and opened his briefcase on the dresser. "I don't know how much help this will be, Nick. He looks half-dead already."

He pulled out four vials and syringes. He filled each with one of the vial solutions and then headed for the bed. He glanced at the guards. "You need to hold him down."

"He's chained up," one of the guards said.

Zeke glared. "Did I stutter?"

Four guys held Knox's limbs as he injected him

with each of the four needles.

Scarlett gulped back the knot in her throat. She'd given up on crying. That shit wasn't helping Knox. She needed answers. "Now what?"

"Now, we wait," Zeke replied.

"What did you give him?" she asked.

"A cocktail of things. Basically, if he comes back after all that, he'll be really different."

"Different how?" Nick asked.

"I've been testing a new drug that gives my specimens the same strength as a shifter, without the animal. I gave him that. I also gave him adrenaline to wake the wolf if he's in there or speed his heart rate to get some kind of reaction from him." He put the vials away along with the needles. "I gave him something that will help regenerate his wounds, if he can get his mind to focus on them it."

"And the last one, what was it?" Shani asked.

Zeke took his glasses off and started wiping them. "A cocktail of alpha shifter DNA I replicated."

"You can't make an alpha," Nick argued.

Zeke shrugged. "Try telling that to my experiments. We'll find out soon enough if I can or not. I discovered that alpha shifters have a higher recuperation speed. More strength. And bigger bodies than all other shifters of their kind."

Scarlett glanced at Knox. He wasn't moving, and for all she knew, he had moments left. "What alpha shifters did you replicate?"

Zeke grinned. "A few of the top ones. If this works the way it's supposed to, he'll either be a multi-shifter or one of the animals will take control and lay claim on his body."

Scarlett gasped. "When will we know if it's working?"

Zeke raised his slim shoulders. "In the lab, sometimes it took days, other times moments before I saw results. I'm doing something I've never done. I have no idea what's going to happen."

Nick sighed. "Okay. We'll keep him guarded at all times." He turned to Shani. "You should go home. Get some rest."

She nodded. "Mom's with the kids, but I do want to check on them."

"Hey, is there anything to eat in this place?" Zeke asked. "I had to leave my lab before I got a chance to eat dinner."

"Yeah. Come with me. I'll take you to the kitchen," Nick said. "Let's go, love," he told Shani.

Shani gave Scarlett a hug. "Have faith. He'll be okay."

Scarlett squeezed her hand. She turned to the bed and pulled up the closest chair and sat, watching Knox for any change. People filed out of the room. The two guards in the room with her glanced at each other.

She said, "You can wait outside."

"It's probably best if we stay here," one of the men replied.

She bared her teeth at him. "I can take care of myself. Wait outside."

The guys walked out behind the others. Finally, she was alone with Knox in the bedroom. One of the many bedrooms in what she now knew was his mansion. The party had quickly come to an end once he'd been attacked. Everyone had been sent home, but no one knew why.

She gazed at his features. Knox. This was why she hadn't wanted to bite him. What the hell was he doing in the forest? Whom was he with?

She swallowed hard at the lump in her throat.

"I'm sorry," she whispered. "I shouldn't have left, but I didn't want to hurt you." She pushed away the urge to cry. He didn't need that. She had to be strong. For him. "I've never wanted a man the way I do you. Earlier tonight, I almost lost control of my lioness." She pulled the chair closer until she was right next to the bed, able to touch his unmoving hand. "I wish I could go back and stay."

Fuck. This was some bullshit. She dropped her head on her hand covering his. If he died—no, he wouldn't die. He couldn't. Her lioness rejected the idea. He was hers. Knox was a genius in investment banking, but she knew there was a lot more to him than that. She wanted to get to know the rest of him.

"What am I going to do?" she whispered.

A soft grunt replied. She jerked up in her seat and glanced at him. Her jaw fell open as she watched his body transform. His already tight abs became more defined. His arms and shoulder muscles bulked. His hair grew and so did a beard.

She glanced down, tugging at the bandage she'd put on his deep chest wounds. They were gone. He was once again smooth and muscular. A lot more muscular than before. Flinging off the blanket covering his legs, she watched them grow big and powerful.

Oh, hell. Her gaze strayed to his groin. That had to be some kind of joke. There was no fucking way his cock was growing before her very eyes and he wasn't even conscious.

"Fuck!"

NINE

Knox's body was on fire. A wolf paced inside his mind, hungry for something. He inhaled and knew then what he was hungry for. The animal bonded with him. There was a strange ability to communicate. Somehow, they both wanted the same thing. Her.

He opened his eyes and followed the delicious scent of his woman. "*Mine.*"

She jumped to her feet and rushed back, away from him. He didn't know why, but her actions excited him. "Knox?"

He tugged at the bonds and wondered why he was chained up. The last thing he remembered was standing outside the bedroom after she left. He frowned. A piece of his memory was missing.

"You smell so fucking good, Scarlett. Let me taste you," he growled.

He growled? He'd never growled in his life. That had to be the animal in him. The wolf told him that yes, it was him giving life to new characteristics in Knox. The first was his need to mate Scarlett. The second was his desire to get her naked and under him. Next was the dominance trying to assert itself as he tugged on the chains. They squeaked as he pulled.

Her eyes widened. "Knox, stop it. You need to get checked out."

He yanked again. His cock hurt. He wanted Scarlett so fucking bad. "You can check me out, beautiful. I've got something that hurts just for you, baby."

"Really, Knox?"

He took in her sexy scent and pulled harder. The chains popped off the wall. He jumped to the middle of the bed. He'd never felt so fucking alive in his life. Everything looked better, brighter. Shit, but her smell. "Take that off or I'm ripping it off you."

She licked her lips. The scent of her arousal drove the wolf inside him insane. "Cut it out!"

He tugged off the bandage on his arm and glanced at his hands. They slowly shifted into massive wolf paws. Holy fuck. This was better than anything he'd ever expected. Humanity had never been a question to him, but he'd known as a human, it would be impossible to get a girl like Scarlett. She was strong and he wasn't. The fact she let him fuck her told him she didn't care how much of a human he was, but she'd been afraid to hurt him.

"I'm so fucking hard for you, baby."

She gulped and glanced at his rock hard erection. "Oh, boy."

"You ready for me to fuck you into the next room, Scarlett? I know that's exactly what you want."

"Nick!" she screamed. "He's up! I mean, awake."

In ten seconds flat, the room was full of people. Nick, Zeke, and four guards rushed in.

"Whoa!" Zeke yelled. "Let me get a look at him." He pulled out a stethoscope, flashlight, and syringe. He stepped next to Scarlett and Knox growled.

"If you value your life, move away from her," Knox told Zeke.

Zeke frowned, glanced at Scarlett and then nodded. "All righty then."

He walked around to the other side of the bed. "Knox, you remember me?"

He nodded. Images of college and living in a dorm with Nick and Zeke flooded his mind. Sights, sounds, and smells crowded his brain as he tried to remember their past. "Zeke Redell."

Zeke grinned. "That's right. I just need to listen to your heart and get some blood, my friend."

Knox glanced at Nick. His best friend was staring at him intently. His wolf didn't like the lion in Nick. So far, the animal hadn't posed any issues, but Nick was still his best friend. This could be a problem.

"You have to show him you're in control," Nick said. "You control the wolf, not the other way around."

"That's right," Zeke agreed. "Start now, or you'll never get the animal to do what you say."

"He doesn't scent like a regular wolf shifter," Nick told Zeke. "Why?"

Zeke stabbed a needle into Knox's arm and started drawing blood. "He's been injected with enough different drugs to mess with anyone's scent. He'll need a few days before you know what he will smell like."

"How do you feel, Knox?" Nick asked, worry evident in his voice. His fear carried to Knox's side of the room.

"I don't know. I was in a world of pain and suddenly I had this wolf telling me to wake the fuck up."

Zeke nodded and finished drawing blood. "That's what I was hoping for. What else?"

"I feel like I should be jumping off the roof or running in the forest."

"That's the adrenaline I gave you," Zeke said. "I needed to make sure your heart sped up so you wouldn't go into a coma or die."

"What else do you feel?" Scarlett asked.

Knox met her gaze and held it. "I feel like these people need to go and you need to stay."

TEN

Scarlett could have creamed her underwear at that moment. The way Knox told her he wanted everyone gone sounded so dominant, she had a hard time keeping herself from getting wet.

"Sex really isn't advisable at this time," Zeke said, glancing back and forth between her and Knox. "We don't know what else will happen with him."

"Knox," Nick started, "you've been through a lot, but you've also had a lot done to you. We don't know what side effects the drugs Zeke used on you will have."

Knox finally glanced away from her and nodded at Nick. "What do you want me to do?"

"We need to keep you under observation. I know it's not ideal, but we have to," Nick told him. "I can put guards on you, or you can stay here and make it easier for them and us."

He glanced at her again. Fuck, that look of pure ownership was going straight to her dreams that night. "I'll stay here. If she stays, too."

She glanced at Nick. He raised a brow. Right. Okay. Hell yes, she wanted to stay, but she didn't want to be a burden. "I'll stay, Nick. I can guard him."

"I'll need full access to him the entire time," Zeke said excitedly. "This is the biggest breakthrough I've had since I started messing around with shifter genome."

"Are you all right to stay here?" Nick asked her. She saw the way he stared at her. He was worried about her safety. He shouldn't be. If only she had explained to Nick how much she'd been fighting her attraction to Knox. Maybe then he'd understand why it nearly killed her to see him bleeding to death.

"I'm fine," she declared. "There's still the threat of the men who came earlier to the party. We have no idea what they wanted or why they were here."

"You're right." Nick turned to the other guards. "I want you and the others to circulate and keep an eye on the area. I'm not sure what's going on, but this doesn't feel right to me."

It didn't feel right to her, either.

"I just need a few minutes with Knox. I have some questions to ask him," Zeke said, rushing over to his briefcase and pulling out a pad and pen.

She motioned for Nick to follow her outside. They walked down the hallway, a few levels down to the ground floor, and to the farthest side of the house, away from extra ears.

"What do you think?" she asked him. She wanted to believe Knox was going to be okay, but she'd scented the same thing Nick had. He didn't smell like a regular shifter. That meant they had no idea what they were dealing with.

"I don't know. At first, I thought Zeke could help him heal, keep him alive." He turned to face her. "Did you see what I saw up there?" Those chains were high-capacity and bolted. Not just that, his physique. He's clearly bigger and strong. Really fucking strong."

She nodded. She shouldn't feel so excited about all the stuff Nick was saying, but she was. This was Knox. For so damn long, she'd worried about him breaking and now he was probably the strongest shifter she'd ever seen.

"The glow of his animal was off, too."

She frowned. "What do you mean?"

"His eyes. Did you see them?"

Dammit. She missed something? She'd been so involved with how domineering his look was, she hadn't paid attention to his animal's glow. "No. What did you see?"

"A wolf's glow is usually yellow. His glow was blue."

That was unusual, seeing as his eyes were brown to begin with. "I don't understand."

"A blue glow isn't common in land shifters. They're air shifters."

She bit her lip. "But remember how Zeke said he used all kinds of shifters? What if this is the one trait he picked up from an air shifter?"

Nick rubbed his jaw. "It's possible."

She opened the fridge and pulled out two bottles of water, handed one to Nick and opened the other. After a few gulps, she sat on one of the bar stools by the kitchen counter.

"Nick, what else is worrying you?"

"Tonight's event was guarded because he had so many influential people here. In order to get in, everyone had to have an invitation."

Shit. "So you mean to tell me those guys were possibly with someone?"

"Yes. The fact they used hunter's block tells me they knew other shifters would be here." Nick gulped down the water in his bottle and set the empty plastic on the counter. "There's something we aren't seeing or don't know."

"We'll need to question him. Find out what he remembers." She cleared her throat. "I can do that. I can talk to him. Perhaps if I ask casually, he'll give me more information."

Nick sighed. "I know you're a grown woman and used to being in dangerous situations," he said, "but I don't think you should get involved with him."

"Nick—" she growled.

"I mean for right now, Scarlett. I wasn't telling you what to do. I just want to know what we're dealing with here. If he goes berserk and tries to kill one of us, I won't have him near you. Do you understand?"

What he said made sense, but in her heart, she knew Knox would never hurt her. Her lioness would put her life in his hands. "I'm an adult with special ops training."

"Give it a few days. Don't do anything drastic," Nick told her. "Keep it in your pants. Wait until all the drugs work themselves out of his system and we see if there are any side effects to him being turned into an alpha versus being a naturally born one."

She gave a sharp nod. "Fine. But only because I want what's best for him."

Nick pulled her into a hug. "I know you do. If this works out, maybe you'll stop denying what you feel."

She reeled back and blinked at him. "How did you know?"

Nick grinned. "I'm your brother. Besides, the only reason I asked him to get you a job with him was because the first time you were in the same room when he came to dinner, you made it damn uncomfortable to sit there while you were thinking whatever it was you were thinking."

She laughed and slapped him on the arm. "Nick! You're not supposed to notice that stuff."

"Too fucking bad. I barely touched my food that night."

She shook her head and pulled away from him. "I'll try to keep my hormones under control."

He gave a soft sigh. "Please do."

ELEVEN

Scarlett carried a plate of food to Knox's room. She figured with all the crazy shifter stuff happening to his body, he was probably starving. The moment she walked in, he jumped up and marched toward her. He took the tray out of her hands and curled a hand around her neck, pulled her to him, and kissed her until she couldn't remember her name.

The kiss was hot, hungry, and possessive. He growled as he took her lips, pressed his body into hers and squished her between the dresser and his hardness. At first, she'd been stunned, but her lioness reveled in the touch and she quickly pushed back, thrusting her tongue into his mouth and rubbing with his.

Her pussy slickened. She wanted so much

more than they could have at that moment. Nick's words came crashing back to her like a bucket of cold water.

She pulled away from the kiss, gasping for air and met his gaze. She saw the blue glow in his eyes now. The rumble in his chest made her belly quiver and her legs shake. Fucking hell, he was sex on a stick. If he'd been hot as fuck as a geeky human, as an alpha shifter, he was making her pussy catch fire, and he hadn't even touched it yet.

"No, but I will."

She blinked. "Will what?"

"Touch it. Soon. Very fucking soon, sweetheart."

Holy crap. He'd read her mind. Shifters didn't do that until they were mated. How was that possible? He only grinned and pressed another kiss on her lips before stepping back.

"Are you hungry?"

He turned and slid a hot glance down her body. "Starved."

She would never survive the night if this kept up. "I meant for food."

Zeke was writing furiously on a desk and table. She ignored him and took the tray to the bedside table. "Eat."

"You and Nick shouldn't worry," Knox said. "I'm fine."

She pressed her lips together. "I'm sure you are, but Nick is concerned for your health."

He cut up the steak she'd made him and ate faster than anyone she knew. "I'd never hurt you. He should know that. You know that."

"What?" She frowned. "Why would you say that?"

"Nick told you he worried I'd hurt you. I'd never touch you in any way other than to make you come."

Ah, fuck. This man was going to need a muzzle. How was she going to keep her girl parts dry if he continued to remind her about making her wet?

"You heard us?"

He nodded, ate the last of his food and drank the water bottle. "Every word."

She gasped. "But we were on the other side of the house. On the first level. Nobody, shifter or human, could hear that."

He winked at her. "I'm no ordinary shifter, sweetheart."

Something else to consider. "What will we do about your work?"

"I have an office here we can work from. I can access all my files and keep clients informed via email."

She moved the tray back to the dresser. "Zeke?"

Zeke turned to her as if he'd just noticed her there. "What?"

"Do you still need him?"

Zeke shot to his feet. "No. I'm going back to the lab. Gotta check out his blood and make notes on his file." He packed up his stuff and walked to the bedroom door. "Let me know the moment anything changes."

She nodded.

"I'll be back tomorrow for more blood and more questions," he said and walked out, shutting the door behind him.

She turned to face Knox and gasped when she realized he was a foot in front of her. "How the hell did you move so quickly and quietly?"

He gave her a wicked grin. "Stealth."

Dick. "All right, you need to get some rest."

He raised a hand to her face. "I know what you're trying to do."

She laughed. "Oh, yeah? What's that? Because I don't have a fucking clue."

His lips lifted. "You don't want to want me, but you do."

If only that were her only problem. "You've been through some serious shit, Knox. We have to make sure you're okay."

"When I prove I'm fine, you won't stop yourself any longer and will follow your animal," he demanded.

She cocked her head. "You got real bossy all of a sudden."

He pulled her into his arms. She probably could have pushed away easily, but she needed this. Needed him. She wanted badly to hold him, just hold him. And tell herself everything was going to be fine. "I'm more than bossy, love."

She knew that. He displayed alpha traits left and right. She ran her nails into his hair. It'd gotten longer since his change. Gone was the impeccable haircut he usually kept. In fact, all his features had changed. The soft, smooth face had transformed into something harder, rougher. "I'm going to get some sleep."

He stroked his fingers over her cheek as if feeling it for the first time. "Your skin's so smooth. I love it."

"Thank you, Knox. You need rest."

He sighed. "Maybe. The wolf has gone quiet."

"Knox—"

He kissed her. This time slowly, savoring. Their lips brushed repeatedly. Then he slid his tongue over her lips, pushing into her mouth and curling over hers. The kiss was more exploratory than demanding. He searched for her weak spots and once he found them, he used them to his advantage. Every moan and whimper was followed by a second and a third. It was as if he were learning Scarlett.

Her legs were ready to buckle when he finally broke their kiss. She imagined dragging him to the bed and begging him to make her his next meal.

"If you don't want us to go any further, you have to go," he said. "Your scent is killing me. It's making it damn hard to control myself," he snarled. "All I can think about is fucking outside, in nature, naked. I want you slick and wet, under me, when I make you mine." He inhaled her scent and his glowing gaze made her press her legs together. "I'm going to have you. Outside. Naked. Screaming my name."

She gulped and hurried to the door. "Call me if you need me. I'll be in the room two doors down."

She didn't bother waiting for him to reply. Instead, she shut the door behind her and ran for her room. Nick had been right. They had to keep their hands away from each other until they knew if anything else was going on with Knox. As it was, she knew nobody who could read minds or hear conversations at the distance he had.

Hopefully, they'd be able to focus on his work while Nick tried to find out more about the people who attacked him. Knowing those assholes were out there and could do that to anyone made her want to rip someone's face off.

Nick would find them. That's what he did best. She went into her room and stripped, rushing in to take a quick shower. After her shower, she changed into a pair of shorts and a tank top from the clothes she'd tossed into her overnight bag when she got the call from Nick.

Sleep was harder to come by. Her lioness kept reminding her that Knox was hers. And that none of her previous arguments were valid any longer. He was now a shifter. The last thing she had to worry about was breaking him in bed. Oh, good god. Why did she go there?

This new version of Knox in bed with her was so not what she needed to think about. She could already imagine him ripping her clothes off and fucking her into the headboard. It might be the highlight of her entire adult life.

TWELVE

Early the next morning, Knox leaned against Scarlett's open bedroom door, watching her sleep. He wanted to crawl into bed with her, let her body curl around him and maybe then he'd be able to quiet the animal. His mind was running a million miles an hour. Already the thirst to run outside and let the wind hit his face, let the animal loose and hunt, were driving him insane.

He couldn't stop the building need to have her. A driving lust that demanded she be his. He burned for her. There was a growing possessiveness that she be his mate and then all would be right in the world. The feelings didn't worry him. He'd wanted Scarlett since the moment he saw her. Now if only they'd hurry up and let him have her. He knew he wouldn't be able to last much longer.

There was something else. Something he didn't know how to explain. A new pull inside him. He went back to his room. Everything looked so differently now. He didn't even need his glasses anymore. It was like high definition twenty-four seven.

Zeke and Nick were in his guestroom, waiting for him. It was funny that they had not taken him to his own bedroom only a few doors down. In a way, he was glad. He didn't need Scarlett seeing that side of him. The comic books in pristine plastics. The DC comics movie collection. Hell, his cheeks flamed at the thought of her seeing his action figure collection. He'd have to man up.

"What's going on?" he asked Nick, noticing his friend's tense stance.

"My lab partner," Zeke shouted. "He stole everything. The serums, your blood and my research."

Nick turned to face Knox. "If this gets out, you will be targeted. The government will want to cut you up in pieces and see how they can put you back together."

Zeke's face paled. "He didn't know what I was working on. Our lab is so big, but I think he overheard my call and must have gotten curious."

"Don't you keep that kind of stuff under lock and key?"

Zeke winced. "Yes, but I guess with all the years we've worked together, he figured out my passwords."

Fucking hell. Knox met Nick's gaze. "There's only one thing to do. Find him."

Nick nodded. "I've got my men on it."

"I want to help," Knox stated. "I know I can be useful."

"Are you crazy?" Zeke argued. "We can't let you out in the general population without knowing what else is going on with you."

Knox growled and took a step towards Zeke. Zeke blanched and moved to use Nick for cover. "Tell him, Nick."

Nick stared at Knox for a tense second before shaking his head. "We need all hands on this."

"You're making a mistake," Zeke warned.

"Then it's my mistake to make," Nick threw back. "Now tell us everything else we need to know about this guy."

"He lives in a tiny ass apartment down the street from the lab." Zeke paced the room. "I went there but it was empty. Like he'd hightailed it out of town in a rush."

Nick snorted. "No kidding."

"He's got family," Zeke glanced at Nick. "I already told you about them."

"My men are checking them out, Knox," Nick told him.

"What else? Goals? Dreams? Perfect places to vacation?" Knox frowned. "Banking information?"

"What?" Zeke cried. "I don't fucking know, dude. I have been up to my eyeballs in serums and haven't had human interaction with anyone in months until you guys."

Knox rolled his eyes at Zeke's rambled excuses. He'd been the same way at one point, though. Not really socializing much. Which was surprising when his biggest client made it a point to tell him his daughter liked Knox. Soon after, he'd started dating Lisa and when they decided to become a couple, Scarlett came into his life. He'd never been able to have sex with Lisa, not once.

His every waking thought had been consumed by Scarlett. He was glad he'd broken things off with Lisa. There was really nothing left for them.

"I'm going to my office. I need to see if I can look into your guy's banking history," he told Zeke and Nick. "Send Scarlett my way."

"Wait," Nick yelled as he headed out of the room. "Are you sure about this?"

"What else is there?" He met Nick's gaze with his own frustrated one. "If I can find out his money or other things, I can figure out where he could be. Or what his plans are."

"You can do that?" he heard Scarlett ask behind him.

"I'll give you a call the moment I find something. If you need me, you know where my office is," he said and turned to her. "Let's go."

THIRTEEN

Scarlett didn't get a chance to ask what they were talking about. She was dragged off by Knox down the hall. They ran down two flights of stairs and through another hall before they reached a massive library. He opened doors at the back of the room that led into a large private office.

The place smelled of Knox. Clearly, this was where he spent his time when he was home. He shut the door and pushed her against it, reminding her vividly of their time in the guest room.

"Good morning, beautiful," he murmured and kissed her lips, softly at first and then with more possessiveness. There was no holding back. She kissed him with the same amount of desire and need she sensed from him.

He rained kisses over her lips and jaw, taking her earlobe between his teeth and sucking hard. “I’ve been dreaming of fucking you against a door again.”

Good god. The guy just didn’t stop. She let out a slow breath and cupped his face in her hands. “Soon.”

Lying wasn’t an option. The minute they knew he was going to be fine, she’d get him naked so fast, his head would spin.

“Not soon enough,” he growled and gave her another kiss before tearing himself away.

She watched him hurry around his desk, his fingers tapping on keys and booting the computer system.

“So what don’t I know?”

“Zeke’s lab partner stole his research. I’m hacking his bank account and computer to see where he went.”

She gasped.

He glanced up from his computer and raised his brows. “What?”

It dawned on her there was a lot she didn’t know about him. “You can do that?”

He turned back to his keyboard. "Yeah. When I was in college, I worked at a big banking company that paid me to hack into their competitor's programs to get the latest information on what they were planning or working on."

Her jaw dropped. "But that's illegal."

He shrugged. "Tell that to a kid who needed tuition money. At the time, my parents said if I wanted to go to college, paying for it was my problem. They were hippies, so it wasn't something they really cared about."

She couldn't see Knox being part of a hippie family. He was too numbers involved, and by the looks of his office, secretly obsessed with comics and comic book movies. Nothing about him screamed flower child.

Then again, the idea of Knox, big, geeky Knox with a tie-dye shirt and daisy crown made her snort a giggle.

"What are you laughing at over there?"

"I thought you could read my mind."

He gave a raspy laugh. "I can, but I'd rather you tell me instead of stopping this to look inside your head."

She glanced at the rows of bookshelves with different comic characters, memorabilia, and action figures. The whole office was like a giant toy store exploded. "You have a thing for comic book characters, I see."

She walked to one shelf with multiple versions of the same guy. "Who is this?"

He raised his head and glanced at her. "Doomsday."

"I don't recall hearing his name before."

He chuckled and continued clicking keys. "He's not really a good guy."

Interesting. She continued down to another row. "Now these guys I recognize. Joker and Harley Quinn. The craziest couple ever." She turned to him and frowned. "Why would you dedicate a full shelf to them?"

He sighed. "Each shelf is divided by my favorite characters. At the top are collectibles. In the middle are comic books. Below are movie memorabilia."

The whole room looked like a collector's dream. She rushed to the other side where she saw a figure that looked somewhat familiar. "This guy looks like Iron Man, but I can tell he's not."

"No, he's not," he said and continued clicking.

She slapped her hands on her hips and growled. "Well, who the hell is he?"

Without looking up, he answered. "Sinestro."

She frowned. "Another bad guy?"

"Yes."

"I didn't realize you liked them so much. Whatever happened to Captain America and Thor?"

"They're pussies," he growled.

She choked on her laughter and walked back to him. "They are not! I happen to like Iron Man."

He shrugged, his brows low in a fierce frown as he stared at his screen. "He's okay, but they're Marvel. I'm a DC fan."

"What does that mean?"

He stopped and glanced up at her. His eyes widened. "You're breaking my heart here, love."

"Oh, cut it out. You're lucky I know any of them. I'm not really into comic books, but that Robert Downey Jr. in *Iron Man* is too tempting to ignore."

He gave a rough growl, his gaze back on the screen. "I'm warning you."

She stuck her tongue out at him, knowing he wasn't even looking at her. "I don't know what the big deal is anyway."

He inhaled hard. "You're right. There is no big deal. The bad guys are the best. End of story."

She rolled her eyes and went to stand by him.

"What are you doing now."

"Zeke gave me the guy's name and address. I was able to get his personal information from his work file at the university."

She pulled a chair up by him. "You hacked into the school?"

FOURTEEN

Scarlett couldn't believe her eyes.

"Yeah. Then I used his direct deposit information to find out his bank. I got into the bank and I'm looking at his latest transactions. I'll look at his credit cards next. See where they've been used."

Holy shit. If she'd wondered about his intelligence before, she didn't any longer. Knox was really fucking smart. She glanced down his intense face to his neck, to his T-shirt. That's when she realized it read $E=MC^2$.

"Why are you staring at my T-shirt?" he asked, writing something on a pad before going back to clicking keys furiously.

"I hadn't really seen you in anything other than a dress shirt before," she gulped.

His bright blue eyes rooted her to the spot. Blue eyes, no longer brown. "I normally wear comic stuff. You may as well know now. As for this shirt, it was the first I grabbed. Do you know what it stands for?"

"Energy something or other."

He grinned and shook his head. "E represents energy. M represents mass and C represents light."

"Right. Like that tells me the secrets of the universe," she replied sarcastically. "I'm not the genius between us."

"All it is saying is for a specific amount of mass, if you multiply it by the speed of light squared, you get its energy equivalence."

She yawned. "Bored. Now tell me what you're doing with..." she glanced at the paper next to him, "Francis Souza." She snorted. "Seriously? His name is Francis?"

"Yeah, goes by Frank. And I am now looking at his credit cards. He rented a car; a charge came through ten minutes ago from a gas station on I-95 down near Richmond."

She jumped to her feet the same time he did. "That's hours from here."

He nodded, grabbed an empty duffel bag, threw the laptop on his desk into it and turned to her. "Let's go. We don't have time to waste."

She ran beside him, down the hall to one of the back entrances to the mansion. "Where are we going?"

"I sent Nick the latest information. He should be coming down the other side of the house and meeting us outside. We have to hurry if we want to get to Francis before he reaches whoever he is planning to sell that to."

"We don't know that he's doing that, though," she said once they reached the backyard. "And how the hell are we leaving?"

"Yes, we do know. His phone records indicate he's been talking to a number registered to a military general and a second number to a known black market bio weapons seller."

She stopped in her tracks. "You got all that while I was looking at your toys?"

"Yes." He stripped off his shirt, jeans, and shoes, handing them to her. "Shove this in my duffel."

She cleared her throat and started tossing his clothes into the bag. "As much as I love seeing you naked, I don't think now's the time—"

"I got your message," Nick interrupted. "You sure about this?"

"He always told me he knew people in the Department of Defense, but I thought he was just talking out of his ass," Zeke said.

"What the hell is going on?" Scarlett snapped. She turned to Nick. "Start talking, now."

"When I injected Knox, I knew the possibility that he'd have more than one animal to shift into existed. He says another has spoken to him and he's ready to let him out."

"I thought you said it was bad to let him out into society. All that crap about not knowing if he would go postal and shit," she snapped.

Zeke cowered away from her. "Yes, but we need to get Frank before he tells anyone about my research."

Knox backed up until he was a good distance from them. Nick grabbed her hand. Then she watched Knox shift into a massive eagle many times the size of any she'd ever seen in the wild. His talons were the size of her face.

"Oh, my god," she whispered.

"Jesus," Nick mumbled.

Knox's eagle spread its wings to the tune of at least twenty feet. The damn thing was the size of a small plane.

"*Come with me*," Knox spoke into her mind. She threw the duffel over her shoulder and ran.

"What are you doing?" Nick ran after her.

"He needs back up. While I agree we should use his bird, someone has to go with him to neutralize the threat. I've done this kind of stuff with you many times, Nick." She climbed on the eagle's back, holding on to his neck.

"I'm calling some guys I know in the DC area. We'll get you back up right away. Knox got us a license plate so we'll send someone to get him, too. In case you don't get there fast enough." Nick had his phone in his hand as he spoke.

They took off, flying high and fast into the clouds. She was glad for her lioness. She dug her claws into the eagle's feathers and it allowed her a safer hold.

"Why didn't you say something about the eagle before?" she asked.

"I didn't realize what he was. He just showed up this morning, wanting to communicate."

"Are there others?" she asked, her gaze on the buildings and houses that looked toy-sized.

"Other what?"

"You know what I mean, Knox. Don't play dumb. Other animals that you haven't mentioned."

"It's possible. I've had some strange sensations, but I guess I'll know when they decide to connect."

There was a long pause before she spoke. *"I'm*

sorry I wasn't there for you, Knox."

"Don't—" he interrupted her.

She closed her eyes for a second, pressing her cheek on his soft feathers. *"If I hadn't been such a coward about my feelings and stayed with you, you'd never gotten hurt."*

"Look where we are," he said as he soared higher into the clouds. *"If I were still human, we wouldn't be able to do this. You'd be scared to hurt me."*

He was right, but that didn't make her feel any better.

FIFTEEN

Knox didn't like taking Scarlett into any kind of dangerous situation. By the time they arrived at Richmond, Knox had a feeling they were cutting things too closely. He landed in the back of a rental car lot. The sun was setting and so they were easily covered under the dark.

They got a car and while she drove, he was able to hack into the GPS of the car Francis had rented and locate him.

Scarlett dialed Nick while Knox tracked their target.

"Nick?" Scarlett spoke into the car's Bluetooth speaker.

"My guys are racing to the house where Knox says the car is parked."

"We'll be there in the next few minutes. What do you want us to do with him?" she asked.

"I called in some favors in DC and was able to delay both people he's supposed to be meeting with. You have about thirty minutes to get in, get our stuff, neutralize him, and let our guys get him."

Knox glanced at his mate. She might not bear his mark yet, but she was his. He worried she might get hurt. He finally understood where she was coming from when he'd been human. But he was a lot stronger than her, and he'd rather handle the guy himself than get her involved.

"Does she really have to be there?"

"Save it, hot stuff," she told him. "I worked with my brother for years. I'm in charge. I've done this countless times and you have no clue what needs doing."

"She's right," Nick added. "Scarlett leads. You follow her orders, Knox. Don't try to be a hero. She knows what she's doing."

The house was off a dirt road. They turned off the car lights so they wouldn't be seen. Francis's car was parked out front and lamps inside the house were on.

They drove to the side and parked behind a barn. His gut told him this wasn't a good idea.

Quietly, they walked up to the house and

peeked through a window. The last thing they needed was to go in and the guy be surrounded by explosives. He inhaled. "I don't smell anything from out here, the wind's blowing the wrong way."

She turned to face him. God, she was beautiful. Her face pursed as she thought. "We have to split up so he doesn't take off on us. I'll take the back and you take the front."

He grabbed her shirt and looked her in the eyes. "Be careful."

She smiled and pressed a kiss to his lips. "You're bossy but so damn hot."

He watched her walk away and headed for the front door. The house had one floor, so nowhere for Francis to run. He waited until he knew she was opening the door before he put pressure on the front lock and broke it, making minimal sound.

Inside, he heard Francis talking to himself.

He waited behind a sofa for the man to come out of the bedroom. His gaze went to the hallway. Scarlett should have come up from the back already. Suddenly, Francis came into the room, dragging Scarlett at his side.

"Come out, don't you think I have cameras in this place?" Francis asked, pointing a gun at Scarlett's side. "You must think I'm really fucking stupid."

He stood up from behind the sofa and watched the pale, pimply man that couldn't weigh more than a hundred ten pounds wet shove a gun deeper into his mate's side.

"You have something that isn't yours," Knox said, staring point-blank at the guy.

He smelled the guy's fear, but that gun helped him feel in control. He didn't know they were shifters.

"Yeah? So Zeke sent you two to get his serum back? Too bad. It's mine now and I'm about to make millions by selling it to two different people."

Knox strode forward. "Can't let you do that, kid."

"Stay right there or I'll shoot her," he screamed. "Don't fuck with me. I'll do it."

Knox met Scarlett's gaze before looking at Francis again. "Then I kill you and the serum still goes with me."

"Over my dead fucking body!"

Scarlett turned, swiping razor-sharp claws over his face. Francis yelled and fired one shot after another into Scarlett's side. Knox was too far to stop it.

Knox's wolf pushed out, taking control. He

shifted and tackled the guy, the gun hand was mangled before he got a chance to shoot more.

In less time than it took Francis to take his last breath, he was torn limb from limb. The wolf clawed at him, bit and ripped him to bite-size pieces.

The door burst open and Nick's guys flowed in. Knox changed to his human self, picked up a bloodied Scarlett and carried her out. "What do I do?"

She winced in pain. "I need to shift."

He saw her struggle to get into her lioness, but once she did, she slumped over and passed out. Nick called in more favors and got them a helicopter to take them home, along with the serums.

SIXTEEN

Scarlett sat up in bed and watched Shani bring her a tray with soup. "You know, I can eat fine. I can even walk if you all would stop babying me."

Shani grinned. "Shush. Knox is beside himself that he let you get shot."

She rolled her eyes. "Newsflash. I did that on purpose. I just didn't expect the asshole to empty the damn clip in me."

Shani flinched. "I know. I've never seen you need so much recuperating sleep before. You were out for three days straight."

She didn't like thinking about it, but that

dickwad Francis had hit some vital organs when he shot her. Luckily, she could shift into her lioness or she definitely would've died.

"How's Nick?" she asked, knowing her brother better than anyone. He was probably holding himself accountable for the fact his men weren't there when she needed them.

Shani grimaced. "He'll be okay. He just needs time to see you'll be fine."

"I already am. If they would stop treating me like I'm going to break, I could get up and walk around and find out what's going on with Knox's tests."

Shani widened her eyes. "Oh! Yes. So apparently, Zeke hasn't found anything to say that he's going to go postal or on a killing spree with dual animals inside him."

Good. She already knew that, but it was nice to hear the words. Maybe now he'd get naked and they could break a bed or two. The mansion had enough of them that it would take a while to go through every room.

"I see your smile." Shani laughed. "I'm going to get Knox, and then Nick and I have to go home." She winked at Scarlett. "Have fun."

Scarlett didn't realize she'd dozed off. She woke to Knox sitting beside her, with his laptop. "What are you doing?"

He raised his gaze from the computer. "Making sure the people meeting up with Francis didn't have anything to go after."

She yawned and sat up. "Hacking stuff again, huh?"

He grinned. "Yes."

She glanced around the bedroom and raised her brows. "Your bedroom, I presume?"

"That's right. I didn't want you far from me." He closed his laptop and set it on the bedside table next to him. "How are you feeling?"

"I'm fine, Knox." She grabbed his hand and pulled him on to the bed where she kissed him. "How are you?"

"Fine, now that you're awake." He cupped her face in his hands. "I'll die if something happens to you."

"Come here," she said and made him get under the covers with her. She leaned into his side and let him hold her. She could think of a time not long ago that she would have laughed at the idea of Knox being in bed with her. "Nothing will happen to me."

He kissed the side of her head and held her

close. "I won't let it."

"I know. You're my sexy Alpha geek."

He barked a laugh. "You have no idea how correct that is."

His cell phone rang and she watched him put it on speaker. "Hey, Nick."

"Knox. I know you're with Scarlett, so I wanted to fill you both in. We got Francis erased. And for the time being, Zeke will have security until we're sure he's in the clear."

"Sounds good. Anything else?"

"Yeah, one more thing. We've searched through your guest records for the night of the party. The only thing we could find is that someone either brought those guys in, or they came through the river side of the house. Otherwise, there would have been no way for them to get in. Not with my guys all over the place."

Knox rubbed his jaw on Scarlett's head. She could feel the tension coming off him in waves. She wanted to make all that shit go away, but knew she couldn't. This was something they had to deal with.

"Thanks. I'll check out the river myself."

"Take care of my sister," Nick ordered.

"With my life," he replied.

She smiled at the definite way he said that. He closed the phone and they were silent for a moment. “Knox, there’s something that’s been bugging me about this room since I woke up.”

SEVENTEEN

"What's that, love?"

"Where's the remote control?" She glanced around but didn't see one. "Don't tell me you're one of those guys who doesn't have a TV in the bedroom. Please tell me you're not one of them."

He chuckled and pressed something above his head. A secret compartment opened and he pulled out a remote. Before he closed it, he hit a button and a TV rose from a giant dresser.

"No, baby. I'm not one of those," he said. "What do you want to watch?"

She snuggled closer into him. "I don't care.

Let's watch your favorite movie."

He laughed. "I doubt you'd find anything I watch entertaining."

"Try me. I've watched a little bit of everything." When he didn't say anything, she glanced at him. "Now you've made me curious. What is your favorite movie?"

"*War Games.*"

She frowned. "I don't think I've seen that one. What's it about?"

"It's old. From the 80s. It's about a teenage hacker that plays tic-tac-toe with an artificial intelligence computer."

She yawned. "Yeah. I definitely did not see that."

"I told you, you might not like the same stuff I do. It's okay, sweetheart. Tell me what you want to see and I got you."

She grabbed his hand and twined her fingers with his. "No. You have to tell me some other movies you like. I must have seen one of them. I watch a lot of movies when I need to relax. I just let them play and zone out." She sighed. "Come on. One more. If I haven't seen it then you can spank me."

He growled. "Don't play, sweetheart. You're still recuperating."

"I'm fine. Now tell me the movie."

"*Spaceballs.*"

"Oh! I've seen that one! It's hilarious. They're making fun of *Star Wars,* right?"

"Yes. I'm surprised. It's old, too." He laughed. "But now I have a question for you."

"Shoot," she said and rubbed his palm with her thumb. It felt so nice to be in his arms and not fighting her attraction for him any longer.

"What kind of movies do you watch?"

"Action. You know, all the Die Hards, though my favorites are *Live Free or Die Hard,* that hacker kid in that one kills me. And *A Good Day to Die Hard*. I love that in those last two, his kids hated his guts at the beginning but by the end they were all *he's my dad,*" she told him. "I'm a sucker for a good ending."

"I should have known, but I didn't take you for an action movie type." He lifted their twined hands to his lips and kissed the back of her hand.

"Oh? What type of movie did you think I liked? If you say drama, I will hurt you."

He laughed and she crawled on his lap, placing her knees to either side of his legs and straddling him.

"No," he met her gaze and inhaled.

At another time she would have worried he could scent her arousal. Not any longer. She didn't care.

"No?"

"I saw you more as a suspense or slasher film where everyone gets killed because they ignore the obvious escape route and do something stupid like head right for the killer."

A smile widened her lips. "Maybe you do know me."

She leaned in, brushing her lips over his, raising her hands around his neck. The kiss was slow, teasing. It was almost as if he were afraid to touch her, but she wasn't having it. Fire bloomed everywhere his hands caressed. He lifted her top off and cupped her breasts.

His hands on her felt good. Warm and fucking perfect. She continued to kiss him, grazing her lips over his beard and down to his neck then back up to his ear. "I want you inside me."

She rocked her hips, rubbing her pussy over his erection. Her shorts and his pajama pants were in her way. He twined his fingers into her hair, holding her still and driving his tongue into her mouth. Finally. That dominance she'd come to expect was there. He took control of the kiss, his lips and tongue stroking and caressing to heat the fire at her core.

She stood on the bed. He grabbed hold of her shorts and yanked them down. Then his pajama pants came off and she was back to straddling him.

"I want your pussy on my mouth," he said.

She bit her lip and raised onto her knees, placing the head of his cock at her entrance. "Maybe later." He slid into her. "Right now, I need you. In me."

She pressed down, her pussy swallowing his cock in one quick slide down. He sucked on her neck and helped her ride him. Every glide brought her closer to the earth-shattering explosion she sought.

He dug his nails into her hips. She raked her own across his back and rocked up and down, back and forth, until her body felt it would break from the inside.

"Knox," she panted.

"I'm here, sweetheart. Let go, I'll catch you."

She didn't know what that meant, but the words had the desired effect. She pressed herself into his chest, her pussy gripping and contracting around his cock. He came in her, his seed filling her aching emptiness with his heat.

He kissed her and changed their position so she was now on her back, her legs wide open. He slid down her body, sucking at her breasts, her belly, and then putting his face in her sex.

EIGHTEEN

Knox sat at his desk when something finally clicked in his mind. That piece of the puzzle from the night he was attacked. Suddenly the image came clear and he saw Lisa.

He picked up his phone and dialed her number but got no answer. Calls to her father went unanswered as well. He had to find out if she was okay. The last thing he wanted was for Lisa to be dead in a ditch somewhere.

"Hey, sexy," Scarlett said as she strolled into his office. "Want to go for a walk? I'm feeling kind of cooped up in here. There's only like twenty thousand square feet to this place and yet I am burning for fresh air."

"Yeah. Just give me one second to send Nick some information." Once he sent Lisa's address and details, he got up from his desk.

They walked out of his office and onto the balcony. From there, they headed into the forest.

"What did you send Nick info about?"

"Lisa."

"What about her?" she asked with a curious tone.

"My memory came back of the night I was attacked. She was being dragged into the forest toward the river. And I ran after them."

She gasped. "Oh, Knox. Do we know if she's okay?"

"I tried contacting her and her father, but nobody picked up." He gulped back the acid in his throat. "I hope she somehow got away."

"Didn't Nick mention the river once? Maybe we should check it out."

They hurried to the farthest side of the house, down the same pathway Lisa had been dragged, until they reached the raging river. He doubted someone could cross that. The only other option was a guest had brought those people with them.

Back at the house, he continued trying to contact Lisa and her father. A call to her father's office told him that Lisa's dad was at his vacation home in the mountains. There was no way to reach him and no other information they could share.

"Uh-oh," Scarlett crossed her arms over her chest. "I know that face. Someone's going to hack something."

He grinned at the way she whispered it. "Babe, we're home. There's no one else here but us. You don't have to whisper."

"So what are you looking for?"

"Just John's mountain home address. I want to go up there and see him. Find out if she's okay."

"Did you call their house?"

He nodded, emailed himself the address, and grabbed her hand. "Yes. Nobody would give me any information other than John was gone. They knew nothing of Lisa."

"Damn."

"Ready for a quick trip?" he asked as they walked outside again.

The sound of helicopter blades reached them. "Thank goodness. I really didn't want to fly on your back again."

He chuckled at her teasing and helped her into the chopper. An hour later, they touched down in the area near the cabin. He gave the chopper instructions to land at the nearest helipad with availability and he'd give them a call when ready to go.

They ran to the front door and knocked repeatedly. Nobody answered.

"Maybe they're out back," Scarlett said and they went around the house.

They walked down a trail. He sniffed but got nothing. His senses told him something was wrong. And a new animal decided to speak to him.

NINETEEN

Scarlett had a really bad feeling about that place. She started to turn and pull Knox with her when a group of men came out of the woods, holding rifles.

"Oh shit. I don't think this is good," she whispered.

She watched a few older men, a younger woman, who she assumed was Lisa, and seven guys point guns at them.

"John, Lisa, I've been calling you both."

"I know," one of the older men replied. "You know, if you had just died when these guys tried to kill you, my life would be so much simpler now."

Scarlett gasped. Her lioness wanted out right now. She'd tear them up and rip their balls off for putting a hand on her man. Knox tensed beside her.

Knox growled. "You did that? Why, John?"

John glared at his daughter. "Because she couldn't get you to fuck her."

"It's not my fault his shit didn't work," Lisa argued.

Oh yeah. She was going to make ribbons out of that bitch's face. Then she was going to lick her paws clean of her blood.

Knox curled his hands into fists. She grabbed hold of one and held tightly. "I still don't understand."

"You know, for a genius, you're damn stupid," John told him. "I wanted you to handle my accounts because I thought you'd be good for my side business. You'd be able to fill in the blanks about where the money was coming from and make it sound legitimate. But you wanted to keep everything by the fucking book." He chuckled. "I know you're great at making money multiply and I wanted that. What I didn't want was you snooping into my shit."

"So Daddy thought if we were in a relationship, you'd be more likely to come to our side and understand that Daddy has some side jobs he gets paid for and all you had to do was invest that money," Lisa told him. "But you always wanted to research where things came from and why he had more money than his accounts should." She shook her head. "Sticking your nose where it wasn't wanted."

"So we had to get rid of you," John said. "No hard feelings, just business."

"Just business," Knox growled. "Your men tried to kill me."

"Yeah, and we still don't know how you came back from the dead," a big guy with a scar on his cheek said.

All their eyes glowed. She knew they were wolves and didn't care that they were outnumbered. She'd stand by Knox and kick all their asses.

"*Don't worry, love. I've got this,*" Knox said into her head.

They readied their guns when Knox shifted. It happened so fast, had she blinked, she would have missed it. One second he was standing next to her, and the next he was a massive blue dragon roaring at the men.

Bullets whizzed by her head. She dodged and flung herself to the ground. Knox stepped in front of her, keeping her safe.

Lisa screamed and ran into the woods. The other men stayed and shot at the dragon. He roared a second time and blew out a plume of fire that lit each one. They ran around trying to tamp out the flames.

Knox's massive dragon blew out another fire breath and continued destroying everything in his wake.

Scarlett rushed into the woods. Her lioness demanded to be let out, so she did a quick shift. She'd been dying to rip Lisa's face off since the beginning.

She sniffed down her prey, listening to footsteps and the sounds of Lisa's cries. In the distance, she heard another roar from her dragon and she knew he had that shit under control.

A curse sounded from ahead. She pawed the ground quietly, taking her sweet time pinpointing Lisa's location.

Hiding behind a thick trunk, Lisa held her rifle out and glanced over her shoulder. "Fucking Knox! He should have died that night."

Scarlett sighted her in and rushed forward as Lisa focused her attention behind herself.

She knocked the woman down, but the rifle stayed in Lisa's grasp. Lisa rolled and raised the rifle to point it at Scarlett.

"I'll fucking kill you!" she screamed. "You

think this is the first time I've fired this at an animal? It's not."

The lioness watched and waited. She saw panic in Lisa's gaze. She glanced around as if scared other animals were going to surround her. The sound of leaves crunching to her left made Lisa swivel the shotgun away from Scarlett. That's all she needed.

She jumped her again, this time knocking the weapon out of her hands and clawing at the other woman's face. Her lioness bit down on Lisa's hands trying to block the attacks. It wasn't long before the wounds killed her, but Scarlett's lioness continued to paw at her until she heard the call of her mate and left Lisa behind.

TWENTY

Scarlett placed her hands flat on the shower tiles and sighed. Hot water dripped down her back, soothing her aching muscles. The next time she raced Knox's wolf, she'd have to get a head start. He was too fast for her.

She washed her body and listened for Knox. He'd told her he was joining her, so she didn't know what the wait was. It was the end of Halloween night, and instead of being at some party, they were finally home after figuring out why Knox had been attacked and making sure those responsible were handled.

After her shower, she slipped a robe around

her body and walked down to Knox's office. He wasn't there. The hairs on her arms stood on end. Uh-oh. What was he doing?

She walked out the door by his office onto the balcony but didn't see him. She did get the distinct feeling he was watching her.

The sky opened up and rain came down so hard, she almost didn't believe it was real.

"I'm coming for you, little cat," he whispered in her mind.

"Did you really just call me that?" She laughed.

"Yes. And unless you plan on giving in quickly, you better run."

She wanted to tell him no, but the lioness wouldn't let her. Instead, she found herself squealing as she ran into the grass, getting drenched from the rain.

Suddenly she was tackled from behind, the robe ripped off her body. They rolled on the grass, the rain falling over them.

He covered her with his naked body. "You're mine now."

She cupped his face with her hands. "I've been yours."

Their kiss was long and sweet. He gave her care, attention, and the usual aggression she was used to simmering under the surface. Water covered their bodies as rain poured. Their hands were all over each other, touching, exploring, as if the first time again.

She pushed him until she was on top. Then she grinned and slowly got up, flipped to put her back to his face, and straddled him again.

"Scarlett," he growled behind her. "I don't know what you're doing, but I fucking love it."

She laughed and scooted back, putting her pussy level with his face, bringing her head to line with his cock.

Her hand grabbed a hold of his hard shaft and pumped him using the rain as lubrication. She lowered her head, took him into her mouth, and moaned. He was so damn smooth, velvety. And hard like steel. She licked and sucked him, using her spit to coat him and jerk him in her grip.

He groaned, his legs tensed and his hand slapped around her hips to pull her down to his face. His tongue flicked into her channel and she moaned around his dick again.

Her head moved faster with each bobbing motion and jerking of his thickness. Rain continued to fall as he sucked on her pussy, making circles with his tongue.

She reared back, almost sitting on his face and groaned. "Fuck, you're really good at eating pussy."

He sucked harder as if her words motivated him. She went back to jerking him and swallowing him down her throat.

A soft growl sent vibrations up her pussy and made her legs shake. She released him from her mouth but continued gripping him hard, gliding her fingers up and down his shaft.

He growled again. The tremor going up her body flung her into an orgasm that caught her off guard. She stopped jerking him and held on, her body shuddering with her release. Loud moans and purrs left her throat.

There wasn't a chance to get her bearings. She was still riding her euphoric wave when he slid from under her and caged her, keeping her on all four. He bit down on her shoulder and plunged his cock deeply into her sex.

A scream lodged in her throat. He slammed his hands on the wet grass to either side of her. "I told you I'd have you like this, outside, naked and screaming my name."

Then he proceeded to fuck all rational thought out of her mind. All she could do was dig her nails into the earth and feel his body taking hers. The rain made it so easy for him to slip and slide over her. Her pussy throbbed with her need to come.

He snarled, his growls and groans growing

louder by her ear. Her lioness loved every fucking second of their mating.

"More...please," she gasped.

"I'll give you more, love," he panted out between harsh thrusts. "I'll give you so much cock, you'll never forget you're mine."

"I won't ever forget," she mumbled, pushing back into each of his plunges.

"So you know every part of you belongs to me," he growled. "From your sweet, hot pussy up to your perfect dick-sucking lips."

She moaned and nodded, pressing back into his kisses and bites. "Yes. But it goes both ways."

His hand gripped at her hip, holding her in place while he fucked her without stopping for even a breath. "I've been yours, sweetheart. Since the moment I laid eyes on you."

She remembered that moment. The second their eyes met and her lioness argued that this was the man they'd been waiting for. That now they could mate and have a cub or ten.

"Oh, baby girl," he breathed by her ear. "I'm going to give you all the cubs you want. I want you barefoot and pregnant with my babies."

She mewled and turned her head to give him better access to lick her throat. "Yes, Knox. I want them. Our cubs."

She didn't expect him to bite down hard on her shoulder, his teeth embedded in her flesh. He continued to drive into her and her hip felt on fire. Before she knew it, she was falling off the ledge and into full blown orgasmic tremors. Her pussy quivered at the same time his cock reared back and then drove deeply. He stopped and she could swear he grew inside her, stretching her channel taut.

She screamed out his name. He growled, still holding her shoulder between his teeth. His cock pulsed and filled her with his cum. Her belly quaked with each spurt of his semen into her sex. They remained locked in place for a long moment. She didn't know how much time passed. Her body had turned into a shuddering mass, her muscles jellified.

He licked at the wound behind her shoulder. She dropped to the grass, only to be turned on her back and him pushing her thighs open to thrust into her again.

"Oh my god, Knox."

He grinned and blue fire lit in his eyes. "I'll never get enough of you, Scarlett. I love you."

She blinked at the slowing rain and stared at him. "What?"

"I love you. From the moment I met you, I knew I had to have you. Then, my heart told me you were the only woman for me."

She twined her arms behind his head. "I love you, Knox. I didn't think I could fall for a human, but I did. It was scary," she finally admitted. "I didn't want to hurt you, or see you hurt."

"I'm not weak anymore."

She grazed her nails over his beard. "I know, but that won't stop me from worrying."

"I don't see why you would worry. I'm never leaving your side." He propelled back, almost out of her completely and drove back in with heart-stopping speed.

She moaned. Legs curled around his hips, she pushed him deeper into her with the heels of her feet. "God, I love you. Even if I don't get the whole DC and Marvel thing."

He chuckled and kissed her lips. "I'll teach you. And then I'll teach our kids."

She whimpered and smoothed her hands over his large shoulders. "I like the sound of that."

"Good, now let's see about giving us some cubs," he said and went back to making her forget her name.

EPILOGUE

"I am amazed," Nick laughed. Knox followed Nick's vision to the other side of his office where Scarlett had their son, Colin, on a blanket staring at the fire.

"What are you amazed about?" God, he loved his wife and kid, or kids seeing they had another on the way.

"You managed to tame my wild sister. It still boggles the mind," he mumbled and shook his head. "I really thought she wouldn't admit to her feelings for you."

Knox watched happiness spread over his mate's features when their son glanced at her with his big blue eyes. She raised her gaze from

Colin and met Knox's.

"I love you," he whispered into her mind.

"I know, my dragon, eagle, wolf mate. I love you, too."

"I wouldn't have let her ignore her feelings." Knox grinned. "I wanted her just as much as she wanted me."

Nick nodded. "Thank god, you were more stubborn than she was."

Knox winked at his mate. She shook her head and turned back to their son. She might not want to admit it, but the night of the party he'd already claimed her, and he'd still been human.

THE END

ABOUT THE AUTHOR

New York Times and USA Today Bestselling Author

Hi! I'm Milly Taiden. I love to write sexy stories featuring fun, sassy heroines with curves and growly alpha males with fur. My books are a great way to satisfy your craving for paranormal romance with action, humor, suspense and happily ever afters.

I live in Florida with my hubby, our boys, and our fur children "Needy Speedy" and "Stormy." Yes, I am aware I'm bossy, and I am seriously addicted to iced caramel lattes.

I love to meet new readers, so come sign up for my newsletter and check out my Facebook page. We always have lots of fun stuff going on there.

Find out more about Milly Taiden here:

Email: millytaiden@gmail.com

Website: http://www.millytaiden.com

Facebook:
http://www.facebook.com/millytaidenpage

Twitter: https://www.twitter.com/millytaiden

SIGN UP FOR MILLY'S NEWSLETTER FOR LATEST NEWS!

http://eepurl.com/pt9q1

If you liked this story, you might also enjoy the following by Milly Taiden:

Sassy Ever After Series

Scent of a Mate *Book One*

A Mate's Bite *Book Two*

Unexpectedly Mated *Book Three*

A Sassy Wedding *Short 3.7*

The Mate Challenge *Book Four*

Sassy in Diapers *Short 4.3*

Fighting for Her Mate *Book Five*

A Fang in the Sass *Book 6*

Shifters Undercover

Bearly in Control *Book One*

Federal Paranormal Unit

Wolf Protector *Federal Paranormal Unit Book One*

Dangerous Protector *Federal Paranormal Unit Book Two*

Unwanted Protector *Federal Paranormal Unit Book Three*

Black Meadow Pack

Sharp Change *Black Meadows Pack Book One*

Caged Heat *Black Meadows Pack Book Two*

Paranormal Dating Agency

Twice the Growl *Book One*

Geek Bearing Gifts *Book Two*

The Purrfect Match *Book Three*

Curves 'Em Right *Book Four*

Tall, Dark and Panther *Book Five*

The Alion King *Book Six*

There's Snow Escape *Book Seven*

Scaling Her Dragon *Book Eight*

In the Roar *Book Nine*

Scrooge Me Hard *Short One*

Bearfoot and Pregnant *Book Ten*

All Kitten Aside *Book Eleven*

Book 12 *(Coming Soon)*

Raging Falls

Miss Taken *Book One*

Miss Matched *Book Two*

Miss Behaved *Book Three (Coming Soon)*

FUR-ocious Lust - Bears

Fur-Bidden *Book One*

Fur-Gotten *Book Two*

Fur-Given Book *Three*

FUR-ocious Lust - Tigers

Stripe-Tease *Book Four*

Stripe-Search *Book Five*

Stripe-Club *Book Six*

Other Works

A Hero's Pride

A Hero Scarred

Wounded Soldiers Set

Wolf Fever

Fate's Wish

Wynter's Captive

Sinfully Naughty Vol. 1

Club Duo Boxed Set

Don't Drink and Hex

Hex Gone Wild

Hex and Kisses

Alpha Owned

Bitten by Night

Seduced by Days

Mated by Night

Taken by Night

Match Made in Hell

Alpha Geek

If you enjoyed the book, please consider leaving a review, even if it's only a line or two; it would make all the difference and would be very much appreciated.

Thank you!